Roman Myths

*Retold from the classic originals
by Diane Namm*

Illustrated by Eric Freeberg

STERLING CHILDREN'S BOOKS
New York

STERLING CHILDREN'S BOOKS
New York

An Imprint of Sterling Publishing
387 Park Avenue South
New York, NY 10016

ISBN 978-1-4549-0611-7

Library of Congress Cataloging-in-Publication Data
Namm, Diane.
  Roman myths : retold from the classic originals / by Diane Namm : illustrated by
Eric Freeberg.
    pages cm. -- (Classic starts)
  ISBN 978-1-4549-0611-7
  1. Mythology, Roman--Juvenile literature. I. Freeberg, Eric, illustrator. II. Title.
  BL803.N36 2014
  398.20937'01--dc23
                                                                    2013026661

Distributed in Canada by Sterling Publishing
ᶜ/o Canadian Manda Group, 165 Dufferin Street
Toronto, Ontario, Canada M6K 3H6
Distributed in the United Kingdom by GMC Distribution Services
Castle Place, 166 High Street, Lewes, East Sussex, England BN7 1XU
Distributed in Australia by Capricorn Link (Australia) Pty. Ltd.
P.O. Box 704, Windsor, NSW 2756, Australia

For information about custom editions, special sales, and premium and corporate
purchases, please contact Sterling Special Sales at 800-805-5489 or
specialsales@sterlingpublishing.com.

Manufactured in China
Lot #:
2 4 6 8 10 9 7 5 3 1
11/13

www.sterlingpublishing.com/kids

CONTENTS

༤

Introduction to Roman Mythology

∽

THE NUMINA

The ancient Romans had a set of gods, just as the Greeks did. Roman gods are similar to Greek gods, but they have different names. The Romans did not originally give their gods personalities the way the Greeks did. Before they adopted the stories about the Greek gods and made them their own, the Romans referred to their own gods as "those who are above." These beings were known as the NUMINA, which means "the Powers." The Romans did not tell stories about the Numina. The Numina weren't even considered male or female. And when the Romans adopted the world of Greek mythology, the faceless spirits of nature they called the Numina became known as the Titans (as they were called by the Greeks).

The Romans used the Numina as a way to take pride in the simple daily acts of their lives. They worshiped the Numina as a way to help keep their households safe. The Romans were practical. They wanted useful gods.

The most important and beloved of the Numina were the LARES and the PENATES. Every Roman family had a Lar, which they believed was the spirit of their ancestors come to watch over them. The Romans also had several Penates, which were personal gods belonging only to the family. Some examples of Penates include a "God of the Home" and a "Guardian of the Food." The Lares and Penates were the protectors of the household. The Romans worshiped these gods in their homes, not in temples. They offered these gods some of their food at each meal.

There were also public Lares and Penates who watched over the Roman city:

SATURN (whom the Greeks called Cronus) was one of the original Numina of Rome. He was considered the protector of the harvest. His wife, OPS (whom the Greeks called Gaea), was a harvest helper. The Romans held the great feast of Saturnalia every winter to give thanks to Saturn for watching over their crops. During that celebration no wars could be fought. Slaves and masters ate at the same table. It was also a time when people gave gifts to one another. This was to celebrate Prometheus's gift of fire to the mortals. Prometheus was Saturn's brother.

JANUS was the god of good beginnings and endings. He was associated with doorways and gates and was always shown looking both ways. The term *Janus-faced* is used to describe someone who is two-faced: someone who lies. When the door to Janus's shrine was closed, it meant that Rome was at peace. If the door to his shrine was open, it meant that Rome was at war. Janus was probably one of the early Roman sky gods. But because he was strictly of Roman origin, he wasn't part of the Dei Consentes (listed below) who were adopted from the Greeks. Janus was honored at the harvest feast so that the coming year would be a good one for the Roman people. The month of January is named for Janus.

There were many other lesser known Numina spirits in ancient Roman times. These spirits did not always have their own stories. Often they appeared as minor characters in the myths.

The following are some of the less important Numina spirits:

FAUNUS (whom the Greeks called Pan) was a prophet who spoke to people in their dreams. He was the king faun who ruled over all the other fauns. Fauns are mythical creatures that live in the woods and mountains. They are half human and half beast. A faun's bottom half looks like a goat, and the top half looks like a man. These creatures also have the horns of a goat. Fauns are the companions of BACCHUS (whom the Greeks called Dionysus), the god of grapes. These creatures spend their days dancing and frolicking.

The CAMENAE were useful and practical goddesses who cared for springs and wells, cured diseases, and foretold the future. They were also known as the MUSES. The Muses were nine spirits honored as the protectors of literature, arts, and science. The Romans assigned the following duties to the Muses: Calliope was the Muse of epic poetry, Clio was the Muse of history, Euterpe was the Muse of flutes and lyric poetry, Thalia was the Muse of comedy and pastoral poetry, Melpomene was the Muse of tragedy, Terpsichore was the Muse of dance, Erato was the Muse of love poetry, Polyhymnia was the Muse of sacred poetry, and Urania was the Muse of astronomy.

The LARES, as was mentioned before, were the unnamed spirits of good mortals (human beings). These were spirits of those who had died and now resided in Hades (the underworld). The LEMURES were the spirits of the wicked who had died. These spirits were greatly feared by the mortals. Then there were the MANES. These were the spirits who were neither all good nor all bad. They interacted with mortals differently, depending on the situation.

QUIRINUS was the name the Romans gave to the spirit of Romulus after his death. Romulus was a mortal and the founder of Rome. The

Romans told stories in which Romulus was turned into a god.

Another one of the Numina was LUCINA, who watched over childbirth. The Romans eventually gave this responsibility to the goddesses JUNO (whom the Greeks called Hera) and DIANA (whom the Greeks called Artemis).

THE DEI CONSENTES

The DEI CONSENTES are the twelve major gods and goddesses who were honored and worshiped in ancient Rome. The six gods are Jupiter, Mars, Neptune, Vulcan, Apollo, and Mercury. The six goddesses are Juno, Minerva, Vesta, Ceres, Diana, and Venus. They all lived together on Mount Olympus. The gods would make trips down to Earth, sometimes in disguise, to live among mortal people from time to time.

JUPITER (whom the Greeks called Zeus) was

the son of the Numina Saturn and Ops. Jupiter's parents, among other Numina, once ruled the world. But then the gods on Mount Olympus, led by Jupiter, rose up against them. As the king of the gods, Jupiter was considered one of the most important gods among the Dei Consentes. He was known as the god of the sky and thunder. Jupiter was in charge of all weather. His special power was the ability to change into any shape or form. The Romans called him Optimus Maximus, which means "the Best and Greatest." Jupiter was worshiped as god of the Roman state in his temple at the Capitoline Hill. He looked after all mortals on Earth and was able to tell them what would happen in the future. His priest, a nobleman called Flamen Dialis, was the highest and most important priest. The color white is associated with Jupiter. All those who served Jupiter wore white. White horses drew Jupiter's chariot, and only white animals were sacrificed to him. The largest planet in our solar system is named after Jupiter.

JUNO (whom the Greeks called Hera) was the queen of heaven and was also considered one of the most important goddesses. Juno was the protector of marriage and childbirth. The month of June was named after Juno and was believed to be the best month for marrying. Juno watched over every female from the moment she was born to the end of her life. After a child was born, the new parents would lay out a table of food and fancy gifts for Juno for a whole week. Women offered sacrifices to the goddess on their birthdays. Juno sometimes was called Moneta and was also the goddess in charge of a household's money. As Moneta, she had a temple dedicated to her in Rome. This temple contained the mint, the place where Roman coins were made.

MINERVA (whom the Greeks called Athena) was the daughter of Jupiter. She was as important a god as Jupiter and Juno. Legend says that Minerva sprouted from Jupiter's head. She was the goddess of poetry, medicine, wisdom, commerce, weaving, crafts, and magic. Minerva often was pictured with her sacred creature, the owl, which is a symbol for wisdom. The Romans also chose to worship her as their goddess of war. She was very important to Roman life.

MARS (whom the Greeks called Ares) was the son of Jupiter and Juno. He sometimes is considered the Romans' favorite god. Mars was the god of war and the protector of Rome. Sometimes called Mars the Avenger, he became known as the personal guardian of the Roman emperor. The Roman soldiers worshiped him. Rome held two festivals a year in his honor. One festival was in October, and it marked the time when the army would put away its weapons for the winter. The other festival was held in the month of March, which is named after Mars.

During this festival, the Romans would ask the god to keep enemies away from their crops and herds. Mars was the father of Romulus and Remus, the founders of Rome.

VULCAN (the god whom the Greeks called Hephaestus) was the son of Juno and Jupiter. He was born with a deformity and was the only god who was not perfect and beautiful. Some stories say that Vulcan was thrown out of heaven by Jupiter, who was offended by his son's deformity. Jupiter made Vulcan the protector of fire. He often was pictured as a blacksmith working over a furnace. The Romans believed that Vulcan's furnace was underneath the volcano Mount Aetna in Sicily. Like many Romans, he was a great builder. He made the grand palaces in the heavens for the gods. He was also the maker of art, arms, iron, and armor for all the Roman gods and heroes.

NEPTUNE (the god of the sea whom the Greeks called Poseidon) was the second son of Saturn and Ops. When Jupiter decided to become king of the gods, he asked his brother Neptune to help him rise up against their father, Saturn. For his help, Jupiter rewarded Neptune by making him god of the sea. But Neptune grew angry at Jupiter, who ruled the other gods harshly. Neptune tried to rise up against Jupiter, but he did not succeed and felt he had to prove that he was more powerful than the other gods. One day he challenged Minerva and Vulcan to a contest to see who could create the most powerful creature. Minerva created a horse, Vulcan created a man, and Neptune created a bull. Neptune's bull chased off Minerva's horse and tore apart Vulcan's man. Neptune proved that he was one of the more powerful gods. The Romans often sacrificed bulls to honor Neptune.

APOLLO (whom the Greeks also called Apollo) was the god of the sun, music, and healing. He was the son of Jupiter and Leto, a mortal woman. Apollo was the twin brother of Diana, goddess of the moon. When Jupiter's wife, Juno, learned that Leto was pregnant, she would not let Leto give birth on dry land. Leto wandered the world until she found a floating island. She gave birth there to Diana and Apollo. When Juno learned of the births, she sent a serpent to hunt Leto to her death. To protect his mother, Apollo asked Vulcan to make him a bow and arrows. With his arrows, Apollo was able to kill and also bring the dead back to life. Apollo often was pictured as handsome and young. He was always pictured holding a bow and arrow or a musical instrument known as a lyre.

DIANA (whom the Greeks called Artemis) was the Lady of Wild Animals, the goddess of the moon, and a hunter for the gods. Like the moon, Diana had a dark side as well as a bright one. She was known as the protector of maidens, innocent youth, and fertility. But she also was known as goddess of the crossways, which were ghostly places of evil magic. Diana was both hunter and protector of wild animals in the forest. She was pictured most often with a deer. The Romans worshiped Diana at a yearly festival in the middle of August called Nemoralia, the Festival of Torches. Diana's worshipers would form a ring of torches and candles around the dark waters of the sacred Lake Nemi. Their lights surrounded the reflection of the moon on the water's surface. They called this Diana's Mirror.

VENUS (whom the Greeks called Aphrodite) was the goddess of love and beauty. Venus was the daughter of Jupiter and a mortal woman, Dione. Some stories say that Venus was born of the foam of the sea. The Romans believed she was the wife of Vulcan. She loved him sweetly in spite of his ugliness. The Romans said that when Venus arrived, she would bring beauty and laughter with her. Neither mortal men and women nor gods and goddesses could resist her sweet charms. Venus was considered the mother of the Roman people through her son Aeneas. Venus was associated with the myrtle tree and often was pictured with a dove, a sparrow, or a swan.

MERCURY (the god whom the Greeks called Hermes) was the son of Jupiter and Maia, the goddess of spring. Mercury was Jupiter's special "messenger" god, graceful and swift. He wore winged sandals on his feet and had wings on his hat. Mercury held a winged magic wand known as Caduceus that had two serpents wound around it. Mercury sometimes was known as a master thief and was the cleverest of all the gods. Some say that as a baby, he stole Apollo's herds of cattle. Jupiter forced Mercury to return them. One of Mercury's responsibilities was to take care of the dying. He would detach their souls from their bodies and accompany them to the underworld. Mercury also was known as the god of commerce and the market, the protector of traders. Every year the Romans held a festival in his honor on the fifteenth of May (the month named in honor of his mother, Maia). Mercury often was pictured holding a money purse with a goat or a rooster by his side.

CERES (whom the Greeks called Demeter) was Jupiter's sister and the goddess of the corn, summertime, and the harvest. She was the only one of the gods who was kind to all humans. She was involved in the daily lives of mortals. The other gods played tricks on the mortals, but the Romans believed that Ceres truly cared about them. They loved her for giving them the gift of the harvest, their reward for nurturing the soil. They believed she was responsible for teaching humans how to grow, preserve, and prepare grain and corn. She also was credited with making the land fertile to help the plants grow. Her daughter Proserpine (whom the Greeks called Persephone) was kidnapped by the god of the underworld, PLUTO (whom the Greeks called Hades). Beautiful Proserpine had to stay with Pluto for four months of every year. The Romans believed that winter occurred because Ceres was sad about being without her daughter for those months. Ceres often was pictured wearing a garland made from ears of corn, holding a stick or farming tool in one hand and a basket of flowers, fruits, or grain in the other.

VESTA (whom the Greeks called Hestia) was sister to Jupiter, Juno, Ceres, Pluto, and Neptune. She was the goddess of the hearth, which is the floor of a fireplace. In ancient Roman times, the hearth was the symbol of the home. Vesta was an important goddess to the

Romans because every newborn child had to be brought to the hearth before being received by the family. Every Roman meal began and ended with an offering to Vesta. Every city had a public hearth dedicated to Vesta. The fire in it was never allowed to go out. If a new city was created, coals from Vesta's fire were used to start the new city's fire. In Rome, Vesta's fire was cared for by six priestesses known as Vestals. This fire was officially put out and relit every year on March 1. If Vesta's fire went out at any other time, it was considered a bad omen, predicting that disaster would come to Rome. Vesta was also the goddess of bakers. She often was pictured with her favorite animal, a mule. Mules were used to turn the millstone that was used to make flour for the bakers.

ROMAN ORIGINS OF THE MODERN CALENDAR

Why do we call the calendar a calendar? The Romans called the first day of each month *Kalendae* or *calends*. This is where we get the word for our modern-day calendar. Originally, the Roman calendar started the new year in the month of March. But Julius Caesar introduced his calendar in 45 B.C.E., and the leader of Rome made the first day of January the start of the year.

The Days of the Week

Sometimes the Romans used symbols to represent the weekdays. For example, Sunday is pictured as the sun symbol, and Monday as the moon symbol.

Sunday means "Day of the Sun." This day was named in honor of Apollo, the sun god.

Monday means "Day of the Moon." This day

was named in honor of Diana, the goddess of the moon.

Tuesday was called *Dies Martis*, or "Day of Mars," in ancient Rome. The word *Tuesday*, as we now call it, comes from the Old English for "Tiw's Day." Tiw was the god of war in Norse mythology as Mars was the god of war in Roman mythology.

Wednesday was called *Dies Mercuri*, or "Day of Mercury," in ancient Rome. In Old English, the day was called "Woden's Day." The Roman god Mercury was similar to the European god Woden.

Thursday is named after the Roman god Jupiter, the god of sky and thunder. Thursday was called *Iovis Dies*, or "Jupiter's Day," in ancient Rome. The Roman god Jupiter was similar to the Norse god Thor. "Thor's Day" became known as Thursday.

Friday was called *Dies Veneris*, or "Day of

Venus," in ancient Rome. The word *Friday*, as we call it, comes from the Old English, "Freya's Day." Freya was the Norse equivalent to the Roman goddess Venus.

Saturday means "Saturn's Day." This day was named in honor of Saturn.

The Names of the Months

Only a few months were named after Roman gods. Most months were named after Latin words for numbers. Two months were named in honor of Roman emperors.

January is named to honor Janus, the god of gates and doorways. He was also the god of beginnings and endings and often was pictured as having two faces looking in opposite directions. In the original Roman calendar, January had twenty-nine days. Once Julius Caesar changed the calendar, January became a month with thirty-one days.

February may have been named to honor Februus, the god of purification. It also may have been named after the festival Februa, which was celebrated in Rome during the second month. This month had twenty-eight days until 45 B.C.E. Julius Caesar declared that February should have twenty-eight days but twenty-nine days every fourth year, or Leap Year.

March was named to honor Mars, the god of war. March was the first month of the Roman year until Julius Caesar made January the first month. March was the month when wars would begin or start again. This month has always had thirty-one days.

April comes from the Latin word *aperire*, which means "to open." The month may have been named April since it is the beginning of spring, when buds and blossoms begin to open. April originally had thirty days, and then it had twenty-eight and twenty-nine days for a while. Then Julius Caesar made April a thirty-day month again.

May was named to honor Maia, the goddess of spring. It also may come from the Latin word *maiores*, which means "seniors," and May was a month dedicated to the elderly. May has always had thirty-one days.

June is named to honor Juno, the queen of the gods. It also may be named after the Latin word *iuniores,* which means "juniors," and June was a month dedicated to young men. June originally had thirty days, and then it had twenty-nine. Julius Caesar declared June to be thirty days again.

July was the month in which the Roman emperor Julius Caesar was born. The month originally was called Quintilis after the Latin word *quint*, or "five." It was the fifth month in the original Roman calendar. Caesar renamed the month after himself in the year 44 B.C.E., the same year he was murdered. July has always had thirty-one days.

August originally was called Sextilis after the Latin word *sextus*, or "six." It was the sixth month in the original Roman calendar. The name was changed to honor the Roman emperor Augustus. Several fortunate events happened to Augustus during this month. August once had thirty days and then twenty-nine days. Julius Caesar made it a month with thirty-one days.

September comes from the Latin word *septem*, which means "seven." It was the seventh month in the original Roman calendar. This month originally had thirty days, and then it had twenty-nine. Julius Caesar declared September to have thirty days again.

October comes from the Latin word *octo*, which means "eight." It was the eighth month in the original Roman calendar. October has always had thirty-one days.

November comes from the Latin word *novem,* which means "nine." It was the ninth month in the original Roman calendar. November originally had thirty days, and then it had twenty-nine. Julius Caesar declared November to have thirty days again.

December comes from the Latin word *decem,* which means "ten." It was the tenth and final month in the original Roman calendar. December has always had thirty-one days.

CHAPTER 1

The Oak and the Linden Tree

Based on the Story of Baucis and Philemon by Ovid

∽

Everything was perfect on Mount Olympus. The gods were always having banquets. The parties had dancing and delicious food that was provided by Jupiter's three beautiful daughters, Euphrosyne, Aglaea, and Thalia. They were known as the Graces and were the spirits of beauty, charm, and joy.

But Jupiter, the king of the gods, was bored. He could not eat another bite of ambrosia, the food of the gods. He would not listen to another note sung by Apollo as he played his lyre. Jupiter shut his eyes tight so that he could not see the Graces do the same dance over and over.

It was all too perfect to bear.

"Mercury!" Jupiter thundered, calling his favorite son. He thought Mercury was the most entertaining and clever of all the gods.

Mercury flew to Jupiter's side as quickly as his winged sandals could carry him. He knew that a call from Jupiter could mean an adventure for him.

"Yes, Father?" Mercury asked.

"Come with me down to Earth. We're going to test the kindness of the people of Phrygia to see if they are worthy of my special protection," Jupiter told him.

The two gods dressed like poor travelers and wandered through the land. Jupiter took the form of an old crippled man. He wore a tattered cloak and used a walking stick. Mercury left his winged sandals behind and went barefoot.

Together they knocked at the doors of hundreds of homes, both grand and poor.

"Please, could you give us a crust of bread or a drop of water?" Jupiter asked.

"May we have a place to rest our feet?" Mercury begged.

"No!" was the answer they got every time. The people of Phrygia slammed doors in their faces. They forced Jupiter and Mercury away from their homes.

"These people are not worthy of your protection, Father," Mercury said. Jupiter was angry. He could not believe that these people were so selfish and mean.

"Let's try one more home," Jupiter said, "or I shall have to take my revenge on these folks."

They came upon a tiny hut with a rickety roof of reeds. The house offered no protection from the weather. It was the poorest and smallest home that they had found. In fact, it was so small and poor that it could hardly be called a house at all. In the garden there was one scrawny cabbage. In the yard there was one bony goose.

"Father, the people of Phrygia refused us at grand homes. They refused us at small homes. The people of this house have barely enough to keep themselves alive," Mercury said.

"All the same, we will give this house a try," Jupiter told him.

Jupiter limped up the crumbling steps and knocked on the door. The door opened wide.

"Hello, strangers," a cheerful old man said with delight.

"Invite them in," an old woman sang from inside the house.

Jupiter and Mercury had to stoop to pass through the low doorway. Once indoors, they saw a snug and comfortable living room. Inside were a kind-faced old man named Philemon and a lively, smiling old woman named Baucis.

"Come in!" Philemon said. "You look as though you've journeyed long."

"You must be weary. Set your feet beside the fire," Baucis offered.

Philemon brought pillows and benches for the travelers to sit beside the hearth. Baucis gave them her softest blanket to cover them.

"You are very kind to go to so much trouble," Jupiter said.

"No trouble at all," Baucis said as she bustled about the cottage.

Jupiter watched carefully as Baucis used the last bit of wood to make a warm, crackling fire.

"You must be hungry," Philemon said. "I'll bring in a cabbage from the garden."

Baucis put a pot to boil on the fire. Philemon added the scrawny cabbage to the pot. With old, trembling hands, Baucis and Philemon set the table for their guests.

Jupiter and Mercury watched in wonder.

From their nearly bare cupboards, Baucis and Philemon set out every morsel of food they had. They placed a dish of olives, a bowl of turnips, two roasted eggs, and two bowls of cabbage soup on the table.

"Please eat," Baucis said to her guests. She looked happy to be able to provide so handsomely for them.

"Please drink," Philemon said to his guests. He proudly offered his very best jug of wine.

Jupiter and Mercury ate heartily. So did Baucis and Philemon. They ate and laughed and told stories long into the night.

Baucis and Philemon were so happy at their supper's success that at first they didn't notice the magic.

No matter how much Jupiter and Mercury ate, there was always food on the plates.

No matter how many cups Philemon poured, there was always wine in the jug.

All at once, Baucis and Philemon went quiet. They looked at each other and began to tremble with fear. The old couple realized that they were in the company of gods.

"Please forgive us for our meager offerings," Baucis said with a quiver in her voice.

"We should have offered you our goose," Philemon declared.

Before Jupiter and Mercury could stop them, Philemon and Baucis hobbled out of the house. Huffing and puffing, they chased the goose around the yard.

"Shall we stop them?" Mercury asked.

"What, and miss all the fun?" Jupiter replied, and smiled.

Jupiter and Mercury watched as Baucis and Philemon made several attempts to catch the wild goose. Soon the old couple was too tired to continue.

At last, Jupiter took pity on them. He asked them to stop and come inside.

"Baucis and Philemon, you are the only ones in this land who have been kind to us. All the others shut us out of their homes. Your neighbors will be punished for their wickedness, but you shall have a reward," Jupiter said. He turned to Mercury. "Show them," he ordered.

Mercury took Baucis and Philemon outside their hut. All they saw was water. The entire countryside surrounding their tiny hut was gone! There were no houses, no trees, and no people. In their place was a great lake. Baucis and Philemon wept for their neighbors, even though those people had been cruel and wicked to them, too. Another amazing thing happened as they wept. Their tiny hut turned into a magnificent temple. It had the whitest marble walls and floors. A roof made of gold gleamed in the sunlight.

"You may ask for whatever you want, and I will grant your wish," Jupiter promised.

Baucis and Philemon were overwhelmed by Jupiter's offer. They whispered to each other. Then Philemon spoke up.

"Let us be your priests. We will guard this temple for you. And let neither of us ever have to live alone. We have loved each other for so long. Promise that we may die together."

Jupiter was pleased. He said to Mercury, "You see, my son, these people are worthy of my special protection after all. And I shall give them what they wish."

And with that, Jupiter and Mercury disappeared.

Baucis and Philemon served Jupiter and cared for his temple for many years. And one day, when they had grown very old, they began to talk about the old days.

They remembered how hard their lives had

been before Jupiter and Mercury had visited them. Something magical happened as they spoke. With every word, a leaf sprouted on their heads. Then bark began to wrap around their bodies. They had only enough time to cry out, "Farewell, my love!" to each other. As the words passed their lips, they became trees. One became a linden tree. The other became an oak tree. But they were still together. They grew from one trunk. Jupiter had kept his promise.

CHAPTER 2

Prometheus and Io
Based on the story by Ovid

∽

Prometheus was Saturn's brother and Jupiter's uncle. In the war between Jupiter and Saturn for control of Mount Olympus, Prometheus had helped Jupiter become the king of the gods. Jupiter loved him for this reason. But Jupiter still became angry when his uncle disobeyed him.

Jupiter had given Prometheus strict orders that only the gods should control the power of fire. But humans begged Prometheus to give them the secret power of fire, and he gave it to them. Prometheus loved mortals.

Jupiter was enraged, but he could not order Prometheus's death. He decided to punish him instead. Jupiter demanded that Prometheus be chained to a rock at the top of a mountain for all of eternity. Through wind and storm, heat and cold, Prometheus stayed chained to the rock. He braved it all without a drop of water or a wink of sleep.

Then one day a strange visitor came. An awkward young cow stumbled over the craggy rocks. She came upon the cliff where Prometheus was chained. A pesky fly buzzed about the cow. It chased and bit her. The cow flicked her tail, twitched her ears, and occasionally kicked and spun. She cried out like a girl who seemed sad and miserable.

The girl-cow stopped short when she saw Prometheus chained to the rock.

"Oh, my goodness! Where am I? Who are you? Why are you chained to a rock? Have the gods punished you as they've punished me?" the girl-cow cried. "I am a girl trapped in the body of a beast. I have nowhere to go. I can only ramble and roam, stumble and fall. I don't know what to do." She sobbed and then threw herself down at Prometheus's feet.

"I know you," Prometheus said, looking closely into the cow's face. He recognized her eyes. "Your name is Io. How have you become a rambling cow?"

Io looked at Prometheus in wonder. "How do you know me? Who are you?" she asked.

"I am Prometheus, the one who gave the mortals fire," he answered simply.

"Oh, good Prometheus! You have such a kind heart. If I tell you everything, would you be able to help me, too?" Io begged.

Before Prometheus could answer, Io's story poured out of her mouth in a flood of words, twitches, and yelps.

"I was once a happy, carefree princess in my father's land. Many young men thought me beautiful. But I never cared for any of them. One night while I was asleep, a cloud spirit burst through my window.

"'Oh, most beautiful princess,' the cloud spirit said. 'Jupiter has seen you, and he has fallen in love. He loves you with all his great powers as a god. He will visit you soon, and you must be ready for him.'

"I thought it was a dream," Io told Prometheus. "But the next day, Jupiter himself came to me. He covered Earth in a thick, dark cloud. I know now that it was so that Juno, his wife, couldn't see us. Jupiter spoke loving words to me. He told me we would have eternal life together. His words were sweet, and his kisses were even sweeter. I fell in love with him. And I thought he loved me too," Io said, shaking her head sadly.

"Then, all of a sudden, the thick, dark cloud

disappeared. Juno had stripped the clouds from the Earth so that she could see clearly what Jupiter was doing. She was in a fiery rage. I heard her say, 'Jupiter, what are you doing on Earth? And where did you get that lovely white cow?'

"I looked down and realized that Juno was talking about me!" Io cried.

"'I've never seen this cow until just this moment, my dear,' Jupiter said to Juno. 'She has been born from the Earth at just this moment,' he lied.

"'I see,' said Juno, clearly not believing Jupiter's story. 'She's a very pretty little cow. Darling husband, would you give her to me as a present? As a symbol of our eternal love?' Juno asked.

"I could say nothing, of course," Io explained. "I was without words and trembling with fear."

Prometheus nodded in sympathy, and Io continued her tale.

"What could Jupiter say? I was just a little cow. If he didn't give me to Juno at that moment, she would have discovered our love," Io explained. "Jupiter gave me to Juno. Then Juno gave me to Argus," Io said with a shudder.

Argus was a horrible creature with a hundred eyes. He was the shepherd of all Juno's herds. He was an excellent watchman. Argus always had some of his eyes open as he slept. He could watch over Io at every moment.

"Jupiter could never rescue me without Juno finding out. All he could do was watch my misery from above. He did not dare come to help me. Jupiter knew that if Juno found out how much he loved me, she would make things even worse.

"At last, Jupiter could bear it no longer. We had to be together again. He sent for his son Mercury, the messenger of the gods.

"'You must find a way to help me rescue Io,'

Jupiter said. 'You must kill the dreaded Argus so we can free her.'

"There is no god more clever than Mercury. He came up with what seemed to me like the perfect plan.

"Mercury flew down to Earth to visit Argus. The god disguised himself as a country fellow who played music on a pipe. Argus heard the lovely music and called to Mercury to come near.

"'Sit beside me on this rock,' Argus offered. 'It's shady and cool in this spot. It's perfect for shepherds.'

"This was what Mercury had hoped would happen. Happily, he did as Argus asked. Mercury played his sweet music hour after hour. He told boring stories. He was hoping to put all of Argus's eyes to sleep at once.

"But no matter how long Mercury played or how many dull stories he told, some of Argus's eyes would stay open while the others slept.

Then at last, Mercury told a slow, long story that did the trick! All of Argus's eyes closed, and he was fast asleep.

"Mercury took his opportunity and killed Argus on the spot. It seemed at that moment I would be free.

"But before Jupiter could return to Earth to rescue me, Juno sent a fly to bite and torment me. I became crazy in my desire to escape the terrible insect. I ran as fast and as far as I could.

"But the fly would not let me stop for food or for drink. It would not let me sleep," she sobbed softly as she finished telling Prometheus her tale.

"I ran as far as I could go. And that has brought me to you," Io added. "Is there anything you can do to help me?" she asked.

Prometheus shook his head sorrowfully.

"I cannot help you, Io," Prometheus told her. "But I can predict your future. What lies ahead for you is more aimless wandering through fearsome lands."

And with that, the fly stung Io so hard that she fled from Prometheus's mountain.

Io roamed the Earth for many years. One day, she reached the Nile River in Egypt. There, far from Juno's watchful and jealous eyes, Jupiter could return Io to her human form.

Jupiter and Io lived happily together for a while. They had a son named Epaphus. Hercules—one of the greatest half-human, half-god heroes—was a descendant of Io's.

Hercules was the one who eventually set Prometheus free from his chains.

CHAPTER 3

Atlas and the Eleventh Labor
of Hercules

⤳

Saturn was Jupiter's father, and Atlas was one of Jupiter's uncles. Saturn, Atlas, and all their brothers were known as the Titans. When Jupiter and his fellow gods declared war on the Titans, the two sides fought bitterly.

The Olympian gods beat the Titans. After the war, Jupiter was quick to punish those who had fought against him. He forced Atlas to hold up the sky on his shoulders.

Atlas held up the sky for many centuries.

Many years later, Hercules was born. His

father was Jupiter, and his mother was a mortal woman. Hercules was half man, half god and had extraordinary strength.

The goddess Juno hated Hercules very much since he was a descendant of Io's. So she ordered King Eurystheus to make Hercules perform twelve impossible labors. Hercules was able to perform the first ten labors. But the eleventh labor was, it seemed, completely impossible.

Hercules was ordered to steal the golden apples from the Garden of the Hesperides. The Hesperides were nymphs who watched over a secret garden of the gods.

"What am I to do?" Hercules wondered. "How can I steal apples from a secret garden? I do not know where it is!"

He thought and thought. Then he knew what to do.

Hercules traveled to the mountaintop where Prometheus was chained. Prometheus knew all the secrets of the gods. Hercules was sure that Prometheus could help him.

"Will you help me find the Garden of the Hesperides?" Hercules asked.

"I do not know where it is," Prometheus replied. "But if you break my chains and free me, I will tell you who can help you and where you may find him."

With several mighty blows, Hercules cracked apart the chains that bound Prometheus to the mountaintop.

"Thank you, Hercules," Prometheus said. Then, as promised, he told Hercules how to find Atlas. Atlas was the father of the nymphs who tended the Garden of the Hesperides. He would help Hercules obtain the golden apples.

With directions from Prometheus, Hercules traveled for days to reach the ends of the Earth. There he found Atlas. The sky sat heavily on the shoulders of Atlas.

"Who are you?" Atlas asked. "Why are you here?"

"Dear Atlas, I am Hercules. I heard how Jupiter punished you. I thought you must be very weary," Hercules said with great sympathy.

"I am," Atlas replied with a heavy sigh.

"You must also be very lonely here at the ends of the Earth," Hercules added.

"It's true. My daughters, the Hesperides, are too busy tending their garden to visit me. And of course, I cannot go to them while I hold up the sky," Atlas told him.

"Perhaps we can help each other out," Hercules suggested.

"What do you have in mind?" Atlas asked.

"I must have golden apples from the Garden of the Hesperides to deliver to King Eurystheus," Hercules told him.

"Impossible," Atlas told him. "Mortals cannot enter the secret garden."

"Exactly," Hercules said. "But, I have the strength of a hundred men. Allow me to hold up the sky in your place. Then you can visit your daughters and bring me the apples I need."

Atlas almost wept with joy at the thought of being able to visit his lovely daughters.

"Are you sure you are strong enough to hold up the sky?" Atlas asked. "If the sky were to fall, Jupiter would punish both of us."

"Let me show you," Hercules said.

Hercules lifted Atlas and the sky on his shoulders. This proved his strength. Then he put Atlas back on the ground.

"Stand right next to me," Atlas instructed Hercules.

With one enormous shrug, Atlas shifted the sky onto Hercules's broad shoulders. Atlas stretched his arms and rolled his neck.

"I'll be back in a while," he assured Hercules.

Hours and days and weeks went by. Hercules

bravely held up the sky. Finally, one day, Atlas returned. He looked happy and rested. He carried with him an armful of golden apples from the Garden of the Hesperides.

"Thank goodness you've arrived," Hercules said with a tired sigh. He was more than ready to return the sky to Atlas's shoulders.

"Not so fast," Atlas said, stepping aside. "I have given this a great deal of thought. Here is what I propose. I will deliver the golden apples to King Eurystheus, and you shall continue to hold up the sky."

Hercules thought for a moment. This was a tricky situation indeed.

"That is a very generous offer," Hercules replied. "That will be just fine. Do me one small favor," he asked.

"Of course," Atlas said with a smile.

"I had not expected to hold up the sky for the rest of my life. Please would you take it for a moment so I can get a cushion for my shoulders?" Hercules said.

"That seems only fair," Atlas agreed. So Atlas stood next to Hercules. Hercules gave the sky back to Atlas.

When Hercules was sure that the sky rested safely on Atlas's shoulders, he knelt to pick up the golden apples.

"What are you doing?" Atlas cried.

"I have set the world straight. Everything is in its right place. And now I really must go!" he replied. Hercules was gone in a flash.

All Atlas could do was sigh.

CHAPTER 4

Romulus and Remus

༄

Long ago in the Italian city-kingdom of Alba Longa, there lived a good king named Numitor with his lovely daughter, Princess Rhea. King Numitor's brother, Amulius, was an evil man. Amulius overthrew King Numitor from his throne. He then banished Numitor from the kingdom and forced him to live in the caves on the outskirts of the city. The new, evil king told Numitor he could never come back.

The new king, Amulius, was afraid that Princess Rhea would have sons who could take the throne back from him. So he imprisoned Princess Rhea in the Temple of Vesta. Anyone in the Temple of Vesta was not allowed to marry.

Mars, the god of war, heard about this injustice and vowed to set things right. He visited Rhea and gave her twin infant sons. They named the twins Romulus and Remus. King Amulius soon found out and ordered the boys killed. Mars and Rhea decided to hide the twins from the evil king.

They placed the infants in a small wooden canoe and set them afloat on the Tiber River. The babies floated along the river for quite some time. At last, they washed up on the shore. Without their mother or father to care for them, the babies began to cry. Their little voices were heard by a nearby she-wolf that had just given birth to wolf pups of her own.

The she-wolf, a favorite animal of Mars, approached the tiny canoe with caution. If the creatures in the canoe were dangerous, she would not let them hurt her pups. But when the she-wolf peered into the canoe, she saw the two screaming, helpless babies. Her heart melted. The she-wolf gently carried them back to her den. There she cared for them as if they were her own pups.

A woodpecker, one of Mars's favorite birds, lived near the wolf's den. He spotted the two infant boys. The bird offered to help the she-wolf care for the babies. The woodpecker brought them food when the she-wolf was too busy.

When the twin boys were toddlers, they ran through the forest and fields with their brother-wolf pups. The boys ran as fast as their chubby little legs would carry them, but they never could keep up with the pups.

One day, when the wolf pups had left the boys far behind, a shepherd named Faustulus found them wandering in the fields. Faustulus had worked as a young shepherd for the evil King Amulius. He remembered when Princess Rhea had been forced to give up her twins. Faustulus looked closely at the boys. They looked exactly like King Numitor. Faustulus realized that these must be the long-lost grandsons of Numitor. These were the grandsons the evil King Amulius had ordered to be killed!

Since Faustulus had no children of his own, he picked up the boys and brought them home to his wife, Loba. He told no one, not even his wife, who the boys really were.

"Look what I found in the fields, my dear," Faustulus told Loba.

At first Loba could not believe her eyes. Gazing at the boys in delight, she cried, "Sons!"

Loba gave the boys hugs and kisses. Both husband and wife welcomed the boys into their lives. Faustulus and Loba raised Romulus and Remus as if they were their own sons.

The boys were greatly respected by the other children in the village. They were both strong and fearsome fighters. Romulus had his followers. Remus had his own. It was clear that these boys were meant to grow up to become great leaders.

When Romulus and Remus were fully grown, they became restless. They knew they were meant for greater things than the simple shepherd's pastures.

"I want to fight great wars," Romulus told anyone who would listen.

"I want to travel to great cities," Remus would add.

Though it pained him to do it, Faustulus knew it was time to tell the boys the story of how they came to be in his house. He told them how the evil King Amulius had driven their grandfather Numitor into the caves beyond the city. Their eyes grew wide.

Romulus and Remus became angry when they learned about the king's wrongdoings. They vowed to get rid of the evil Amulius so that their grandfather Numitor could be king again.

They said good-bye to the kind shepherd and his wife. They thanked them for all their love and good care. Romulus and Remus then set out for the city-kingdom of Alba Longa.

Finally they reached the castle. Without hesitation, they stormed through its giant doors with their weapons drawn.

"We are the grandsons of Numitor," they both roared.

Amulius grew pale. He trembled with fear as if he had seen two ghosts.

"B-b-b-ut I thought you were—were—dead!" Amulius sputtered in disbelief.

"We both are very much alive! And now you must pay for the wrongs you have done," shouted Remus.

"Amulius. You must go!" Romulus said.

The twins charged toward the evil king. Romulus and Remus attacked Amulius viciously. The evil king had no choice but to flee the castle and his kingdom forever. He feared for his life.

Next, the two brothers searched high and low through the caves on the outskirts of the city of Alba Longa. At long last they found their grandfather, Numitor. The old man's clothes were tattered and torn. He was half blind and living in a cave.

Numitor looked up at the two great warriors standing before him.

"Who are you?" the old king asked, his voice trembling.

"We are Romulus and Remus, the sons of your daughter Princess Rhea and the great god Mars," said Romulus.

"We have rescued your kingdom and driven Amulius away," Remus told him.

"My kingdom is saved?" Numitor asked, not quite believing what he was hearing. "And where is my daughter?

The two warriors shook their heads sadly. "She is gone," they told him sadly. Romulus and Remus patiently explained what Faustulus had told them. Numitor wept as he learned of all that had happened to his daughter and her sons.

"Grandfather, come with us," Romulus urged him. "We will bring you back to your castle, and you shall once again be king," he promised.

The two warriors gently led the good King Numitor out of the darkened cave and into the sunlight. Tears streamed down Numitor's face. He embraced his grandsons and kissed them each on the cheek. Then he slowly walked with them back to his kingdom.

True to their word, Romulus and Remus brought Numitor back to Alba Longa, and he became king once again.

"My boys, it is time for you to find your own cities to rule," King Numitor told them. "You were both born to be kings."

"But where shall we rule?" Remus asked his brother.

"We can build our own city," Romulus replied.

The two brothers roamed the land, looking for a place to rule. Every time Romulus would pick a spot, Remus would argue with him.

"This is no place for a city worthy of me," Remus remarked.

But every time Remus chose a site, Romulus would also argue.

"Build a city here? This spot isn't fit for mice, much less the men who will be my followers," Romulus told him, laughing.

Then Romulus stopped in his tracks.

"I know the perfect place to build a city," Romulus declared. "Our new city should be on the hills above the Tiber River, where the she-wolf saved our lives."

"That is a great place for my city," Remus said with confidence.

"It will be the place for my city, not yours," Romulus shouted.

"Over my dead body," Remus shouted back.

The brothers quarreled for hours. Then they began to fight. As they matched each other blow for blow, it was clear that neither would surrender the site by the Tiber River.

"We will let the gods decide," both the brothers agreed.

Each brother climbed a mountain to see what signs the gods might send them. Remus saw a flock of six vultures soar high above him.

"Surely this means that I am the one to rule," said Remus.

Romulus saw a flock of twelve vultures fly past him.

"It is clear that the gods favor me to rule. I saw more vultures in the sky than you did," Romulus told his brother.

"That means nothing," argued Remus. "The gods want me to rule."

"No, they don't," Romulus shouted.

At once, Romulus collected a group of followers to help him build his city on the hills that sloped over Tiber River. Romulus and his followers began to build the low walls of his city.

Remus, who had not been able to get anyone to help him, watched as Romulus slowly built.

Remus laughed at his brother.

"Those walls are so low and weak. Your city will be easy to invade," Remus told Romulus. "I don't need to build another city. I'll just wait until you are done building and take over yours."

"You will never take my city from me," Romulus shouted. In a fit of fury, he rushed at

Remus, striking him to the ground. Romulus killed Remus instantly.

Then Romulus returned to building his city just the way he wanted it, without fear that his brother would invade. However, all of Romulus's followers disappeared after they saw him murder his brother. Romulus became an outcast. But he didn't care. He swore to build the city himself.

After he built the city, Romulus realized that he had no citizens to live in it with him. He declared that his city would be a safe haven for anyone who had done wrong, as he had. Outlaws and fugitives who had nowhere else to go flocked to Romulus's new city. Soon it was full of people. Romulus welcomed them all.

Then Romulus named the city after himself. He called it Rome.

CHAPTER 5

Escape from Troy

∽

Aeneas was a man who lived happily in the
city of Troy with his family. He was the son of
the goddess Venus and a mortal man, Anchises.
But Aeneas became a soldier overnight when
the Trojan War began. The conflict started when
Paris, Prince of Troy, stole Helen of Greece away
from her husband, Menelaus. Menelaus was the
brother of King Agamemnon.

Paris greatly angered the powerful king, who
declared war on Troy for Paris having wronged
his brother. All Trojan men were needed to

defend their city. Aeneas was one of them. He became the leader of a mighty group of soldiers.

The Greeks were favored by the goddess Juno. They attacked Troy with a vengeance. Then, after many heated battles, the Greeks pretended to leave Troy. The Trojans thought this meant they had won the war. But the Greeks left a giant wooden horse the size of a ship outside the city walls of Troy. The Trojans thought it was a peace offering, and so they brought the horse inside the city and celebrated their victory over the Greeks. Greek warriors were hiding inside the hollow wooden horse. In the middle of the night, they spilled out from the horse and started the final battle of the Trojan War. They opened the city gates so that thousands more Greek warriors could enter Troy. The city exploded in a burst of flames.

Aeneas's frail father begged him to leave the city with his wife and son. "Leave me, Aeneas,"

he said. "Your destiny lies outside these walls. You are chosen by the gods. You are the son of Venus. Escape so that you may find your future!"

"I won't leave you, Father," Aeneas declared.

Aeneas carried his father, Anchises, on his back. He led his wife, Creusa, and their son through the blazing streets of Troy. During the escape, Creusa and Aeneas got separated. Aeneas searched the flaming buildings for his beloved wife, but he could not find her. She was lost.

With Venus's help they arrived at the shore. A ship was there to take them and many of Aeneas's soldiers away.

"Wait," Aeneas told them.

Once more, he returned to the burning city of Troy to search for his beloved wife. Then he heard her voice.

"Aeneas," Creusa called to him.

Aeneas turned around frantically, but he could not see Creusa anywhere.

"Where are you, my love? Let me save you," he shouted.

"I am past saving," Creusa said in his ear. "I am nothing but ash and dust. You must save yourself," she whispered.

Aeneas blinked his eyes through the smoke and ash that swirled around him. He thought he saw Creusa's ghost before she disappeared into thin air. Aeneas knew he had lost his wife forever. With a broken heart, he returned to the harbor, where the ship with his soldiers was waiting for him.

"Push off!" Aeneas commanded.

"Where shall we sail?" asked the captain.

"Where the wind and the water take us," Aeneas replied. "The gods will guide our way."

Aeneas and his followers set sail for lands unknown. Their ship was whipped by winds and soaked with rain.

The goddess Juno hated all Trojans as much

as she loved all Greeks. She particularly hated Aeneas. Juno vowed to make Aeneas's life as difficult as she possibly could, and so she threw obstacles in his way.

After many long days and nights, Aeneas's ship arrived safely on the island of Crete with Venus's help. But Aeneas and his men were discouraged. They immediately knew that this land was not going to be their home. *Where are we supposed to settle?* they thought. Many thought they would never find a home.

That night, the answer came to Aeneas in a dream sent by Venus.

"We will settle in a land called Italy," he told his followers when he woke up. "Our voyage will be long. The seas we will travel are mysterious and filled with danger. But we will find our home when we arrive on the shores of my dream."

Aeneas and his followers set sail that very day. Juno watched their progress from above.

She would not let Aeneas reach his promised land. Not without a fight.

Soon the sky grew dark. A horrible stench filled the air. Winged creatures with hooked beaks and fearsome claws attacked the crew.

"Harpies!" Aeneas shouted. "Take aim and shoot true," he commanded.

Aeneas and his men shot arrow after arrow, but there were too many harpies.

Suddenly, a fierce wind blew. It guided Aeneas's ship away from the harpies. It was a godly wind. Venus had saved them again.

The ship sailed to a peaceful land, and so the men could rest. Aeneas met a prophet there who told him of the dangers he would face on his voyage to Italy.

"You must not sail to the northern shore of Italy. The Greeks have settled there, and the goddess Juno protects them. Sail south, to Sicily. Avoid the waters guarded by two monsters:

Scylla, which sucks ships into a deep abyss, and Charybdis, which smashes ships with a powerful whirlpool," the prophet warned.

Aeneas did as the prophet told him and sailed for the southern shore. But the prophet did not know about the trouble that Juno had in store for Aeneas.

A great storm struck just as Aeneas came to the shore of Sicily. The storm was so big that there has never been one larger. The giant waves drenched the stars in the sky. The spaces between the waves were so deep that the sailors could see the ocean floor. This was clearly bigger than a regular storm. In fact, it was a storm of Juno's anger.

Juno especially hated Aeneas because the Fates had declared that one day Aeneas's descendants, Romulus and Remus, would found the city of Rome. And Juno knew that one day Rome would conquer Carthage, the city she loved the most. Juno knew she could not go against the

Fates. None of the gods had the power to do that. But she tried her best to drown Aeneas.

Juno went to Aeolus, King of the Winds.

"Good Aeolus, send your strongest winds to sink the Trojan ships of Aeneas," Juno asked. Aeolus agreed.

But Neptune, Juno's brother and the god of the sea, got in the way of her plans.

Neptune was taking his daily nap when he heard the waves crashing and the winds whistling. "How could this be? I did not order a storm today," he said.

Neptune stirred from his sleep. He saw the giant storm that was not of his making. He flew into a rage. How dare someone start a storm without his permission!

Neptune learned that Aeneas and the Trojans were caught in the storm. He knew from this that the storm had been created by Juno. But Neptune was always careful when dealing with

Juno. Her temper and cruelty were legendary. To avoid an argument with Juno, Neptune scolded Aeolus instead. After all, Aeolus worked for him, not for Juno.

Fearing Neptune's anger, Aeolus calmed the seas at once.

But once again, Aeneas was faced with a bitter loss. Aeneas's old father, Anchises, did not make it through the storm. The old man had died from exposure to the rough weather. Aeneas was distraught.

Aeneas sailed to the nearest city to rest and recover. By a twist of fate, that city was Carthage. It was the very city Juno wanted to protect. Juno smiled a satisfied smile.

Juno had a plan to save Carthage and change the fated future.

The grand city of Carthage was ruled by the beautiful Queen Dido. Dido's husband, the king, had passed away. She was a widow. Juno planned to make Aeneas and Dido fall in love. Then Aeneas would settle in Carthage and never make it to Italy.

But Venus, the mother of Aeneas, discovered Juno's plan. At first, she thought to stop Aeneas from falling in love with Dido. She wanted her son to find his way to Italy, which was his destiny. But then Venus decided to beat Juno at her own game.

Venus went to Jupiter.

"Dear Brother, King of Gods and Men," Venus began. "You have promised me that my son Aeneas would have descendants who would one day rule the world. But instead. . ." And here her words caught in her throat. Her lovely eyes filled with tears.

"Aeneas is almost ruined. He has met with only hardship. His wife and father are dead. He may never reach Italy after all," Venus sobbed.

Jupiter wiped away her tears.

"Sister, I assure you: all promised for Aeneas will come true. His descendants will create a city called Rome. They will have an endless empire. I know this will come to pass. The Fates have declared it," Jupiter said.

Venus was uplifted by this news. To make sure that Jupiter's prediction would happen, she asked her son Cupid for help.

"The Fates have decided that Aeneas will find his way to Italy," Venus said to Cupid. "He will not lose his heart to the beautiful queen Dido. But Dido's heart is another matter. Many powerful men have asked for her assistance. She has refused them all. Dido must fall in love with Aeneas hard. She must love him enough to help repair his ships. He must be able to sail at a moment's notice. For my plan to work, Dido must love Aeneas to her death," Venus told Cupid.

"Mother, have no fear," Cupid said to her. "Just one of my arrows will set her heart on fire.

She will love Aeneas madly from the instant she sees him."

Venus was happy. Now she had to make sure that Aeneas and Dido met in the proper setting.

Aeneas left his ship to explore where he had landed. He felt defeated and alone. He had no idea where he was.

Venus suddenly appeared before him. She was disguised as a huntress.

"Where am I?" Aeneas asked the disguised goddess Venus.

"You are just outside the city of Carthage," Venus replied. She told him the best way to get to the city. "Queen Dido will be of great help to you and your crew. You must visit her."

Aeneas set off for Carthage at once. Venus wrapped him in a thick mist so that nothing could prevent him from meeting the queen. Aeneas walked through the busy streets of Carthage as though he were invisible.

Aeneas came upon a magnificent temple at the end of a grand street. At the top of the steps he saw Queen Dido. He was dazzled by her appearance. Dido was as beautiful as a goddess.

The mist surrounding Aeneas disappeared.

Cupid took careful aim and fired a love arrow straight into Dido's heart.

As soon as Dido caught sight of Aeneas, her heart began to flutter. She thought he was the most handsome and noble man she had ever seen.

Dido welcomed Aeneas to her city. She planned a giant banquet in his honor. Aeneas told Dido about his desperate journey, the loss of his wife and father, and his search for a home. Dido knew what it was like to be without a home. She had fled her own homeland once upon a time.

Perhaps Dido would not have fallen in love with Aeneas without the help of Cupid's arrow. But Dido's love for Aeneas was enormous. She wanted to give him everything. And she wanted nothing except his undying love.

This had been Venus's plan all along. She knew Aeneas would now benefit from all that Queen Dido had to offer, and he did not have to give Dido anything in return. The plan was working!

"My city is your city," Dido told him. "You shall be my husband and rule by my side. Your followers will be our distinguished guests. I will help you repair your fleet of ships so that we may travel the world together."

Dido arranged a variety of amusements for Aeneas and his men. She begged him to tell her of his adventures over and over. She never grew tired of hearing about them. Aeneas had a powerful and beautiful queen to provide for his every wish. He had no desire to set sail for Italy.

At the same time, Juno also thought that *her* plan was working. She was keeping Carthage safe by holding Aeneas back from sailing to the Italian shore. If he never reached Italy, his descendants would never create Rome. Then no Romans would destroy Carthage.

Meanwhile, Venus wasn't worried at all. She knew her brother Jupiter would keep his word. He would make sure that Aeneas left for Italy. Through Dido's love and generosity, Aeneas would have everything he needed.

Soon Aeneas's ships were repaired. They sat at the shore, ready to sail away from Carthage. When Jupiter saw that Aeneas delayed, he sent Mercury to give Aeneas a message.

Mercury located Aeneas in the middle of an admiring crowd of entertainers, jugglers, and fools. Aeneas wore a gold-threaded cloak on his shoulders. He carried a magnificent sword studded with gems.

"How long will you waste your time here on foolish matters?" Mercury whispered, unseen, into Aeneas's ear. "Your followers await your orders. Your ships lie ready to sail."

Aeneas turned to see who had spoken. There he saw Mercury, the winged messenger god, standing before him.

"Jupiter, the ruler of heaven and earth, has sent me to you," Mercury told him. "You must leave Carthage at once. Find the kingdom that is your destiny. Jupiter insists that you go to Italy."

Mercury vanished into thin air.

Aeneas was overwhelmed by this godly message. He was determined to obey Jupiter. How could he disobey the king of the gods? But how would he ever say good-bye to Dido? She loved him, and he had come to rely on her for everything. He had to go in secret. Aeneas gathered his followers in a private location.

"We will prepare to leave the city of Carthage at once," he told the men. "Say nothing about this to anyone else."

But one of Dido's maids overheard them talking about Aeneas's plans to leave. Then she quickly returned to Dido's castle to tell her mistress what she had learned.

Dido could not believe that Aeneas really meant to leave her. She felt absolutely betrayed. She was beyond hurt. It felt as though Aeneas had stabbed her through the heart with a knife. She went to him at once.

"Have I not loved you well?" Dido asked.

"Indeed, you have," Aeneas answered.

"Have I not given you my kingdom and more?" she cried.

"You have," Aeneas replied.

"So how can you leave me? I cannot live without you," she sobbed.

Aeneas's heart grew cold.

"Jupiter commands me to leave. I must obey," Aeneas said. "We are not married. I am free to leave whenever I choose. I owe you nothing."

Aeneas's words chilled Dido's heart.

"You owe me everything!" Dido spit the words at him.

Filled with sorrow and shame, Dido knew she could not bear to live without Aeneas. She died that day of a broken heart.

Aeneas and his men sailed away from Carthage the same night.

CHAPTER 6

The Golden Bough

⤳

After sailing for many weeks, Aeneas's ships finally reached the Italian shore. Aeneas remembered the words of the prophet he had met when he began his journey.

"Seek the cave of the Sibyl of Cumae," the prophet had told him. "She has deep wisdom and can tell the future. The Sibyl will know where you must go and what you must do once you reach your destined land."

Aeneas set out to find the Sibyl's cave. Before too long, he did.

The Sibyl's cave was dim and had a low ceiling. Aeneas bent and walked carefully over a floor littered with cracked shells and broken twigs.

"Who goes there?" a creaky voice called out.

"Good Sibyl," Aeneas greeted her. "It is I, Aeneas, son of the mortal Anchises and the goddess Venus." Suddenly the cave was flooded with candlelight.

"Well, Aeneas, son of the mortal Anchises and the goddess Venus. What do you want?" the Sibyl asked.

"I have come to you to learn my fate. Jupiter commanded me to reach this land. I am meant to create a great empire. But what am I supposed to do?" Aeneas asked.

The Sibyl held her clawlike hands to her forehead and closed her squinty eyes.

Aeneas watched her wrinkled face for an answer or a sign. At long last, the Sibyl opened her eyes and fixed her gaze on Aeneas.

"You must ask your father, Anchises," the Sibyl said.

Aeneas's heart filled with despair.

"But I cannot. My father is gone. He died during a great storm," Aeneas cried. "There must be something you can tell me."

"Your father is the only one who can help you," the Sibyl replied.

Then the candlelight began to grow dim.

"But wait! How can I reach him?" Aeneas asked. "He is no longer in this world!"

"Then you will have to travel to the world in which he lives," the Sibyl said.

"To the underworld?" Aeneas asked in a hushed voice.

"Yes, you must travel to the underworld ruled by Hades," the Sibyl said. The candlelight was now barely visible. Aeneas's heart sank.

"Good Sibyl, is there any way you can help me?" Aeneas spoke into the darkness.

"If you bring me the golden bough, I will take you to the underworld," the Sibyl crowed.

"I will bring it to you," Aeneas said eagerly. "Where is the golden bough?" he asked.

"Deep in the heart of the forest, there is a tree with one gold branch. It grows in the center of Lake Avernus," the Sibyl told him. "The lake protects the underworld's entrance. Only those who carry the golden bough may enter."

"How will I find the lake?" Aeneas asked.

"Follow your nose," the Sibyl cackled. Then she vanished into thin air.

The candlelight in the cave flickered out. Aeneas was left in the dark.

Aeneas stumbled out of the dark cave into the bright light of day. He wandered through the nearby forest. There were so many trees. It seemed impossible that he would be able to find one gold branch. Just then, he saw two white doves fly overhead. He recognized the doves as the birds of Venus, his mother. She must have sent them to lead him to the golden bough.

Aeneas followed the flight of the doves. He soon came to a foul-smelling lake. The doves soared through the sky and landed on a tree in the center of the lake. Aeneas could see a glint of gold at the top of the tree. It was the golden bough!

Aeneas slogged through the murky, smelly waters of the lake. He finally came to the tree in the center. He slowly climbed up the thick tree trunk. His skin was coated with slime, and his clothes stuck to his skin. At long last, he got to the top of the tree. He reached for the golden bough and

Snap!

Aeneas broke off the golden bough. With a happy heart, he climbed down the tree and raced back to the Sibyl's cave.

"Good Sibyl! I've brought you the golden bough. Now please take me to my father,"

Aeneas said. He had done what the Sibyl had asked of him. She now had to bring him to the underworld.

"Be warned, young man. Entering the underworld is simple. Its dark doors stand open all night and all day. The tricky part is coming back up to the sweet air of the world," she told him.

They journeyed together to the cavern entrance. It was very dark. Aeneas gripped the golden bough in his hand.

"Wait!" the Sibyl called out. "Before we enter the underworld, we must offer up a sacrifice to Hecate. She is the dreaded goddess of the night. We must make her happy so that she will not get angry. We don't want her to tell Hades that some of the living are about to trespass in his world of the dead."

The Sibyl placed their sacrifice to Hecate onto a slab of stone. Suddenly, the earth trembled beneath their feet. Wolves howled in the distance. Other wild animal cries sounded through the darkness.

"Hecate is satisfied," the Sibyl told him. "Follow me!" Then the Sibyl jumped into the hole in the earth that led to the underworld. Aeneas followed her.

They found themselves on a frightening road wrapped in shadows. Aeneas shuddered. He saw horrors to the left of them and horrors to the right. The Sibyl didn't seem to notice or care.

Aeneas had never seen anything like it. There was Disease, Hunger, Revenge, Death, Hatred, and Conflict—they were frightful, moaning spirits with snakelike, bloodstained hair.

Aeneas trembled with fear until they reached a river's shore. A gloomy old man in a rowboat waited there. Aeneas saw a pitiful sight on the opposite bank. There were thousands of shriveled spirits with their arms outstretched. They begged the man in the rowboat to bring them

into the underworld. But the old man, named Charon, permitted only some of them to board his boat. Others he simply denied.

"Why does he not help them all cross into the underworld?" Aeneas asked the Sibyl.

"This is where the two great rivers of the underworld cross," the Sibyl explained. "Those who have not been properly buried may not board Charon's boat and enter the underworld. Their souls are doomed to wander for one hundred years," she added. "Come, let us see if he will take us," the Sibyl said, guiding Aeneas down to the boat.

They were about to board the boat when Charon cried out, "Stop! I do not carry the living. This boat is only for the dead."

"Hold up the golden bough," the Sibyl whispered to Aeneas.

Upon catching sight of the gleaming branch, Charon reconsidered. Without further protest, he allowed the Sibyl and Aeneas into his boat. Charon silently rowed them across the river.

The Sibyl and Aeneas climbed ashore. Aeneas heard a mighty growl. He turned and saw three sets of snarling, dripping teeth. It was Cerberus, the three-headed dog that guarded the entrance to the underworld.

"What do we do now?" Aeneas whispered to the Sibyl.

"Piece of cake," the Sibyl whispered back.

"What?" Aeneas asked.

"Good doggy. . . . Here, doggy. . . . Here you go," the Sibyl cooed. She handed a piece of cake to each dog's head. Cerberus wagged its tail and let them pass.

Aeneas and the Sibyl hurried through the dark, echoing justice hall. This was where souls learned where they had to go. The hall had high ceilings and walls and floors made of black glass.

Then they entered the Field of Mourning. Lovers who had died of broken hearts lived there.

Aeneas spotted Queen Dido in the Field of Mourning beside a myrtle tree.

"Dido, my dearest," Aeneas said. "I didn't know you would be here. How? Why?"

Dido did not seem to recognize him.

"Forgive me, my love! It pains me to see you here. I am so sorry for leaving you the way I did. I no longer know why I did," Aeneas said to her. Tears were streaming down his face. Dido turned away. She would not speak. She would not listen.

"We must hurry," the Sibyl urged Aeneas. They continued on their way.

They reached a spot where the road divided: left and right. Horrid sounds came from the left path—groans, beatings, and chains clanking. Aeneas stopped in fear.

"That road leads to the land of the wicked," said the Sibyl. "There they are punished for eternity. You must hang the golden bough here." She pointed to a wall between the paths. Aeneas dutifully hung the bough.

The Sibyl walked briskly down the right path. Aeneas hurried to join her.

"Where are we going now?" he asked.

"To the Elysian Fields, of course. That is where the right path leads. That is where you will find your good father," the Sibyl told him.

When Aeneas and the Sibyl arrived at the end of the path, they saw a paradise. There were soft green meadows surrounded by lovely groves of trees. Sunlight softly glowed in the sweet-scented air. The Elysian Fields was a place of peace and restfulness. Great people lived there. There were heroes, poets, and those who were kind to others while they lived.

It didn't take long for Aeneas to find his good

father, Anchises, resting in the shade under the most beautiful tree in the Elysian Fields.

"Father!" cried Aeneas.

"Aeneas, my son!" Anchises called out.

They ran to each other with open arms and greeted each other with joy. This meeting between the dead and the living was an incredible and strange surprise to them both. It was proof that even the world of death cannot break the bond between loved ones.

Aeneas and Anchises spoke for hours. They had much to tell each other.

"Let me tell you about your future family," Anchises told him.

He told Aeneas about the Roman leaders who would be born from Romulus and Remus, Aeneas's grandchildren. He advised Aeneas on how to inhabit Italy. He warned him about the dangers and problems he would face. Anchises gave Aeneas the courage and strength to believe that creating the Roman Empire was worth all past and future difficulties.

"Our time here is up, Aeneas," the Sibyl appeared and said.

Anchises and Aeneas gave each other one last long embrace. But they knew they would see each other again.

Then the Sibyl and Aeneas followed the shine of the golden bough through the dark underworld and back into the land of the living. Finally they passed through the gates of the underworld. The air was sweet again. The breezes moved gently through the air. The sun shone on Aeneas's face.

Aeneas turned to thank the Sibyl for her help. But she was gone!

Aeneas returned to his ships with a lighter heart. His father had told him all that needed to be done. That same day Aeneas set out to fulfill his destiny.

CHAPTER 7

Cupid and Psyche

༄

There once was a king who had three lovely daughters. The youngest one, named Psyche, was the loveliest of all. Psyche's beauty and good nature were known throughout the land. People traveled from near and far to gaze upon her with wonder and adoration. In truth, the people treated the mortal woman as though she were a goddess.

"Psyche is the most beautiful creature on the Earth," her many admirers agreed. "She is even more beautiful than the goddess Venus!"

Crowds started coming to worship Psyche. This left Venus's temple cold and empty. The honor and affection that had always been shown to Venus now were directed at Psyche. Venus was enraged.

"How dare she replace me? How can my followers be so stupid as to worship a mortal instead of me!?" Venus fumed to her son, Cupid. Cupid was a beautiful winged creature and was known as the god of love. He used a bow to shoot arrows that made people fall in love with each other. His arrows were so powerful that neither mortals nor gods had any defense against them.

"Who has angered you so, dear mother? How may I help you?" Cupid asked as he and Venus hovered above the clouds. Shaking with anger, Venus pointed to Earth. Cupid's eyes followed the direction of her finger.

"You must use your powerful arrows to teach Psyche a lesson," Venus said. "I want you to shoot an arrow deep into her heart. I want her to fall in love with the most miserable and despicable creature in the whole world," Venus commanded. The clouds parted, and Psyche's beauty shone up to the sky.

Cupid first laid eyes on Psyche at that moment. He fell in love with her instantly! For Cupid, it was as if Psyche were the only creature on Earth. Cupid saw nothing except her soft wavy hair, her rosy-red cheeks, and her perfect smile. Psyche had charmed the god of love himself! Her beauty was so powerful, it was like one of Cupid's arrows. And it had struck Cupid's own heart.

But Cupid did not dare show these feelings to his mother.

"I know you'll take care of this . . . problem," Venus said happily.

Then she kissed Cupid lightly on the head and floated off. Venus was confident that Cupid would quickly ruin Psyche. Of course, she had

no idea that Cupid had fallen deeply in love with the object of his mother's hatred.

Cupid did not want to disobey his mother. But he also did not want Psyche to fall in love with anyone but him. Unable to solve this dilemma on his own, Cupid told his story to Apollo and begged him for advice. Apollo told him just what to do.

Meanwhile, the humans went about their business. Psyche's sisters, both less lovely than she, were splendidly married to kings. But the most beautiful, Psyche, was sad and alone day after day, week after week.

In spite of Venus's orders, Psyche did not fall in love with a miserable creature. She did not fall in love at all. Even stranger, no one fell in love with her. Suitors came and looked upon her in wonder. They worshiped her beauty. But each one passed over her and married another woman instead. Psyche was admired but never loved. Her parents worried that she would never find true love and marry.

Finally, Psyche's father went to ask the advice of Apollo. He traveled to Apollo's temple and sank to his knees.

"Great and mighty Apollo," he began. "My daughter is beautiful, kind, and worshiped by all who gaze upon her. My wife and I are getting old. We want Psyche to be loved and cared for after we're gone. Please help us find her a mate," Psyche's father begged.

There was silence for a moment. Then Apollo spoke words that would chill any loving father's heart and fill his soul with dread.

"Dress Psyche in dark mourning rags. Take her to the highest point of a cliff. Then walk away and leave her alone," Apollo said.

"Please do not ask me to do that!" Psyche's father was most troubled. "What will happen to her?" he asked.

"Her destined husband will appear on that hill. A fearful winged serpent—stronger than the gods themselves—will come and make her his wife," Apollo replied.

"How can you ask this of me?" Psyche's father cried out. There was only silence. Apollo would make no further reply.

In misery, Psyche's father returned to his land. He told his wife and daughter the terrible news. Psyche's mother wept. Psyche begged to stay.

"Once a god has given an order, we mortals must obey," Psyche's father said. His cheeks were wet with tears.

Psyche's mother dressed the girl as though she were preparing her for death. With a heavy heart, Psyche's parents brought her to the top of the cliff.

Only Psyche remained calm and courageous.

"This is my own doing," Psyche told her parents. "All of the attention I received for my beauty was bound to anger the gods, and so I have brought upon us the fury of heaven. I'm willing and ready to pay the price. Leave me. Please know that I'm glad that the end is finally near," Psyche told them, drying her parents' tears.

With grief and despair, Psyche's parents left her atop the cliff to meet her doom. They shut themselves in their home to mourn for her.

Alone in the dark atop the cliff, Psyche wept and trembled. She waited for a terror she did not know.

As she shivered in the night, a soft wind blew. It was the gentle breathing of Zephyr, the sweetest and mildest of the winds. Psyche felt it lift her up. Psyche floated far away from the cliff. She was enveloped in the warm and gentle wind. The wind finally brought her down on a grassy meadow. It was as soft as a bed and was filled with the perfume of flowers.

It was so peaceful a place that Psyche forgot all her troubles. She promptly fell asleep. She awoke to the sound of a river rushing beside her. Psyche was not quite sure what she was seeing. A gorgeous mansion stood on the river's bank. It was ten times the size of any palace she had ever seen. The mansion had pillars of gold, walls of silver, and floors carpeted with jewels. It was fit for the gods!

Psyche looked all around in wonder. She drew nearer to the mansion but saw no one and heard nothing. The place appeared to be completely empty.

Psyche entered the shining mansion. As she passed through the doorway, she heard voices whispering in her ear. She still could see no one. But the words spoken by the voices were crystal clear.

"This is your house now," said one.

"Enter without fear," said another.

"We are your servants," said a third. "Ready to do whatever you desire."

My servants? Psyche thought. She decided to test this out.

"I'd like a bath," Psyche announced.

At once, she found herself in a giant, delightfully warm tub. When she was done bathing, she wrapped herself in thick, fluffy towels.

"I'd like something to eat," Psyche declared.

Quick as a wink, a banquet of the most delicious food appeared on a long table. While Psyche ate, she heard the sweet music of a harp joined by angelic voices singing. Psyche remained alone throughout the day. Her only company was those strange unseen voices.

That evening, Psyche slid into a luxurious canopied bed in the largest of the bedrooms. She lay on the smooth silk sheets. Psyche drifted into the twilight between being awake and being asleep. Suddenly she heard a soft, low voice murmur into her ear. It was her husband-in-waiting. Strangely, she was not afraid. In fact, hearing the sound of his voice made all her fears and doubts melt away. Psyche knew without seeing him that he was no monster or creature to be feared. He was the gentle friend and husband she had always hoped to find.

Psyche woke alone the next morning. The voice of her husband was gone. All day long, Psyche wandered through the empty house alone. She heard only her servants' voices. But again that evening when Psyche was in the twilight sleep, she heard her husband's voice.

"I love you, Psyche. I want you with me always," she heard him murmur.

In the beginning, she was bewildered by the nightly appearance and morning disappearance of her husband. But Psyche kept busy during the day, commanding the whispering servants to do what she desired. The time passed quickly, and eventually Psyche was happy.

But one night Psyche's invisible husband spoke in a serious tone.

"Our lives are in great danger," Psyche heard him say.

"Why?" Psyche asked him.

"Your two sisters are going to visit the cliff where you disappeared. They come to weep for you," the voice told her.

"That is wonderful news. I'll go to them to tell them how happy I am! They will know they do not have to weep," Psyche said.

"No!" her husband's voice interrupted sharply. "You must not let them see you. It will bring great sorrow upon me and will ruin you."

Psyche thought for a moment.

"I will not speak to them. I promise, my love," Psyche said with a sad heart.

Psyche wept the whole next day. She could not bear the thought of her two sisters' sorrow. She was very troubled that she was unable to go to them.

That evening, when her husband returned to her, Psyche was still in tears. Nothing that he said or promised would stop her sobs.

At last Psyche's invisible husband could stand her sadness no longer.

"If you so desire to speak to your sisters, then I will not keep you from it," he said sorrowfully. "Do what you will. But it will mean the end of us one day. This I know," he added.

Psyche's heart was torn. She loved her invisible husband with all her heart. But she missed her sisters desperately.

"I won't let anything or anyone come between us," Psyche promised.

"Then we will let them visit," her husband finally agreed.

Psyche's heart was filled with joy. She could hardly wait for morning to arrive. She so desperately wanted to see her sisters.

"One more thing," her husband's voice whispered. "Let no one persuade you to try to see my true form. It must be enough that you only hear my voice. For if you do try to see me, we will be separated for all of eternity."

"I will do no such thing," Psyche promised. "I would rather die a hundred deaths than be separated from you, my love," she added. "But it will give me great joy to see my sisters once more."

"Then it shall be so," he vowed.

The next morning, the Zephyr wind carried the two sisters from the cliff to the mansion where Psyche now lived.

Psyche ran to her sisters. They laughed and kissed. They hugged and cried. Psyche invited them to come inside the mansion.

Psyche showed them her palace. The sisters

*ooh*ed over the gleaming gold pillars. They *aah*ed over the floor studded with rubies, diamonds, and emeralds. They marveled at the rich banquet and heavenly music.

But something happened to the two sisters while they *ooh*ed and *aah*ed. They grew bitter with envy. They were desperately curious to know who the lord of this magnificent place was.

"Where is your husband?" one sister asked.

"He's away on a hunting trip," Psyche lied to keep her promise to her husband.

When it was time for her sisters to go, Psyche filled their arms with gold and jewels. She asked the Zephyr to take her sisters home gently.

The sisters left graciously. But upon their return home, their hearts burned with jealousy. The riches and splendor of their own palaces were nothing compared with those of Psyche's splendid mansion. Their envy and anger would not go away. The two jealous sisters came up with a plan to ruin the beautiful Psyche.

That night, Psyche greeted her invisible husband with joy. "Thank you, my love, for letting me see my sisters today," she said.

"Now that you've seen your sisters, you must never see them again," he warned.

"But my love, I can never see you either. Must I never see anyone else? Not even my sisters, who bring me such happiness?" Psyche asked, with tears welling up in her eyes.

"I cannot deny you anything. And I cannot bear to see you cry," her husband replied. "You may see them as you wish," he said with a sigh.

With every visit, Psyche's sisters became more jealous and demanding.

At dinner, one sister asked, "Where is your husband this time?"

The other wanted to know, "What does he look like?"

"Is he tall? Is he handsome?"

Psyche avoided their questions. It became clear to the sisters that Psyche had no idea what her husband looked like.

"Is he a hideous monster of whom you're ashamed?" taunted the first sister.

"Of course not! He's just . . . very . . . kind," was the only thing Psyche could say.

"I have heard he is a frightful winged serpent with claws and evil eyes," one sister said.

"And although he may seem kind, perhaps one night he will gobble you up or peck out your eyes," the other warned.

Psyche's heart flooded with terror. Why would her husband never let her see him? She really knew nothing about him. It was cruel to forbid her to see him.

"It's true," Psyche stammered. "I have never seen him. Perhaps there is something wrong. What should I do?" she asked.

"Hide a sharp knife and a lamp beside your bed," one sister told her.

"When he's fast asleep, light the lamp and grab the knife," the second one said.

"Prepare yourself to see the hideous creature by your side," the first sister whispered.

"Then plunge the knife into his heart," the second sister advised.

"We will be nearby," they assured her. "We will bring you home where you belong once he is dead."

Then they left her alone for the night.

Psyche was torn by doubt. What should she do? She loved her dear husband. Could he really be a horrible winged serpent who might peck out her eyes?

That evening, when her husband was fast asleep, Psyche gathered all her courage. She grabbed the knife with one hand. She lit the lamp by her bedside and held up the knife, ready to see a hideous creature by her side. Psyche was shocked by what she saw.

"Oh, my," Psyche gasped. "It is Cupid, the god of love!"

Her husband was the most handsome and gentle man Psyche had ever seen. At first, relief and joy filled her heart. Then she felt ashamed for her lack of faith in her husband.

Psyche moved in closer to kiss the god-husband who lay by her side. She wanted to apologize to him. As she leaned over, some drops of hot oil fell on his shoulder. Cupid, the god of love, jumped as he woke up.

Cupid took one look at Psyche and the lamp. He knew at once what she had done.

"Love cannot live where there is no trust," he said.

And with that, Cupid was gone.

CHAPTER 8

Minerva and Arachne

A long time ago in a small town there lived a young maiden named Arachne. She shared a modest home with her father. Her mother had died when Arachne was just a little girl. The maiden was the most skilled and artful spinner in the land. She became known throughout the region for the beautiful tapestries she wove on her loom.

The nearby wood nymphs came down from their vine-covered slopes to gaze at the silky rainbow threads Arachne would spin. The nearby river nymphs splashed to the shore to see the tapestries Arachne would weave. It was a joy to look at her finished cloths. But the crowds were also mesmerized by the way Arachne would spin and weave.

First she wound the rough purple home-dyed yarn into a giant-size ball. Then she worked the yarn with her nimble fingers. She teased out the clouds of wool, drawing them into long equal threads. She twirled the slender spindle with her skillful thumb. Arachne wove splendid tapestries and delicately embroidered them with her tiny needle.

The crowds were amazed.

"What skill!" someone said.

"What grace!" said someone else.

"The goddess Minerva must have taught her," said another.

When Arachne heard that comment, she stopped spinning and weaving.

"No one has taught me to spin and weave. My tapestries are perfect works of art. Not even Minerva herself could spin and weave as I do," Arachne boasted.

Minerva heard Arachne's words. Her eyes flared. Her blood boiled. Her hair stood on end. How dare a mortal challenge a goddess's skills!

Minerva came up with a plan. She would teach Arachne a lesson that the maiden would never forget.

Minerva disguised herself as an old peasant woman. She gave herself gray hair and carried a walking stick to support her. She appeared in the crowd that watched Arachne at work.

"You spin and weave well, young maiden," the old peasant woman croaked. "You should praise Minerva for your steady eye and light touch," she added.

"I spin and weave with perfection," Arachne replied without dropping a stitch on her loom.

"And I need praise only myself, thank you very much!" Arachne smirked.

The old woman gazed at Arachne with steely gray eyes.

"You should ask Minerva's forgiveness for your lack of humility and your thoughtless pride," the old woman suggested. "If you ask her nicely, I'm sure she'll forgive you."

Arachne turned to the old woman with a fierce reply.

"Be on your way, old woman! No one asked for your advice. If Minerva thinks she can spin and weave better than I, let her appear. Let us compete," Arachne said.

At that moment, with a whirl and a whoosh, the old peasant woman's disguise fell away. Minerva stood before them, tall, strong, and golden haired. "Here I am!" she announced.

All who were there bowed to Minerva in fear and awe. All bowed except Arachne, who stood stubbornly tall. She would not apologize to the goddess.

"Since you will not ask for my forgiveness, let the contest begin!" Minerva declared.

A loom and spindle magically appeared before Minerva.

Minerva and Arachne took their places opposite each other. They stretched out their fine threads over their loom frames. They positioned their spindles. Their hands were ready to weave.

"On your mark . . . get set . . . GO!" cried a voice from the crowd.

They each wove quickly with nimble fingers. Their skill and ease made it seem not like work at all. Arachne wove silky threads of sky blue and copper. Minerva wove her threads of godlike gold and silver. They used a thousand colors. Their fingers flew over their looms with a speed too fast to be seen by the human eye until at last the tapestries were done!

Minerva's tapestry was a heavenly portrait of all the gods and goddesses. It showed them all at their best, performing feats of strength and great courage. Arachne's tapestry was a not-so-heavenly portrait. It showed all the tricks and mean pranks that the gods had played on the mortals.

Minerva appointed the half goddess Envy to be the judge.

"There is such delicacy in the embroidery. I've never seen such perfect tiny stitching," she said about each tapestry.

After hours of close review, Envy was done.

"They are equally magnificent. Both are perfect works of art. You both win!" Envy exclaimed.

"I told you so," Arachne said to the goddess Minerva, smiling.

At the sight of Arachne's smile, Minerva flew into a rage. In one swift motion, Minerva tore Arachne's tapestry to shreds. Then she tied up

Arachne in her own silky threads and hung her from a branch up high.

"From this day forward, you, your children, and all your future generations will hang from a silken thread as you do now," Minerva told her.

Then Minerva sprinkled Arachne with the juice of a poisonous herb. Arachne's hair fell out. Her nose and ears broke off. Her head shrank to the size of a tiny ball. Her body shrank too. Her slender fingers and her legs stuck to the sides of her belly.

"You will spin perfect silky threads made from your spit," Minerva said to Arachne. "And to punish you for your thoughtless pride, you may only weave webs. You shall be a spider for all time!"

CHAPTER 9

Oedipus and the Sphinx

⚬

Long, long ago, there was a great and beautiful city called Thebes. A frightful monster terrorized the city and its people. The creature was a winged lion with the face of a woman. Its wings were as wide as mighty oak trees. Its many teeth were sharp and pointy. It had a deafening roar. This horrible beast was known as the Sphinx. It lay in wait for travelers along the road to and from Thebes. Without warning, the Sphinx would swoop out from its smelly lair, grab an unsuspecting traveler, and fly him back to its lair.

"Answer my riddle correctly and I'll let you live. Answer it wrongly . . . you'll die!" the Sphinx would say, snarling.

No traveler had ever left the Sphinx's lair. The beast would tear its prisoner into shreds and gobble him up right there.

The city of Thebes was in a state of terror. The seven gates to the city were closed. No food came in. No citizens went out. Famine spread across the land.

Things seemed at their worst for the people of Thebes. But then a stranger arrived. He was a man of great wisdom. He had a soul with great courage. His name was Oedipus. At this time in his life, Oedipus was homeless and friendless. There was nowhere in particular he had to be. There was no one in the world who cared where he was.

Oedipus found out about the Sphinx on his travels through the countryside. He heard, too, about the trouble the city of Thebes was having. Oedipus was determined to seek out the Sphinx. He would try to solve the riddle and rid Thebes of the terrible beast.

Oedipus lingered on the road to Thebes. He sat under a shaded tree. He ate a meager lunch of bread and olives.

Oedipus stretched his arms wide and yawned. "I'm not afraid of a ridiculous creature like a Sphinx," Oedipus declared. He did this on purpose, hoping that the Sphinx would hear him.

"Ah, me." He yawned again. Then he lay under the tree and closed his eyes.

The Sphinx watched Oedipus in angry silence. How dare this mortal not be afraid of him!

Finally the enraged Sphinx had had enough of the fearless snores of Oedipus. The creature pounced on Oedipus and dragged him to its lair.

"You foolish mortal! How dare you trespass on my road!" the Sphinx roared.

Oedipus faced the Sphinx without trembling. He could feel its awful breath hot on his face.

"This is not your road, Sphinx. It is the road to Thebes. You should leave this place and these people in peace," Oedipus said.

"It is you who will leave this place . . . in pieces!" cackled the Sphinx.

Then it flared its nostrils. It flashed its eyes. It roared mightily.

"I dare you! Do your worst," Oedipus said. "I do not fear your threats."

"Answer my riddle correctly and you shall live. Answer it wrongly and . . . you die," snarled the Sphinx.

The Sphinx waited for Oedipus to cry out in terror, fall to his knees, or plead for his life. That was what all those who had come before him had done.

"Come on, then," Oedipus said. "I'm listening," he added without breaking a sweat.

The Sphinx thought of its hardest riddle, one it was sure that no mortal could answer. With an evil grin, the Sphinx began.

"What creature goes on all fours in the morning, two legs during midday, and three legs in the evening?" the Sphinx asked. "You have five minutes to think."

Oedipus repeated the riddle to himself.

The Sphinx sharpened its claws.

"What a delightful dinner you're going to make," said the Sphinx.

"Not so fast," Oedipus replied.

Just as the Sphinx was getting ready to strike, Oedipus started to speak.

"The answer is . . . humans!" Oedipus exclaimed. "As babies, we mortals crawl on hands and knees: all fours. As adults we walk upright on two legs. But at the end of our lives, when we're old and frail, we use a walking stick to help us through our days: that's three."

The Sphinx could not believe its ears. Oedipus was right! The Sphinx became angrier than it had ever been before. Its head shook in fury. Its ears began to steam. Its wings began to flap. And all at once, the great beast exploded in a blast of smoke and fire.

The news of the Sphinx's defeat traveled fast through the city of Thebes. The citizens opened its seven gates. They emerged in wonder.

"Oedipus! Oedipus!" the people cheered.

The people of Thebes were very grateful to be free of the terrible Sphinx. They made Oedipus their king at once, and he ruled there happily for many years.

CHAPTER 10

Otus and Ephialtes, Twin Giants

෴

There were once twin brothers who were giants. They were not horrible, ugly monsters with gnarled bodies and knotty hands. Otus and Ephialtes were a rare kind of giant. They were handsome. They stood tall. They were full of charm and grace. These twin giants were the sons of Neptune, god of the sea. Otus and Ephialtes were the nephews of Jupiter, the gods' king. They were important. Or at least they thought they were important.

The two young giants thought the world of

themselves. They believed that they were better than the gods. They played pranks on the gods from a young age. To the gods, Otus and Ephialtes wanted to prove just how great they were.

One day they approached Mars, the god of war.

"Dear Uncle," said Otus. "We worship you and your wisdom in war."

"Would you settle a dispute between us?" Ephialtes asked.

Flattered by their question, Mars was willing to help.

"Ephialtes thinks the best way to capture a prisoner is to bind him with rope and bury him in a hole," said Otus.

"Well, rope unravels. And holes wash away. Over time, your prisoner would get away," Mars told them.

"Exactly what I thought," Otus said with a smile.

Ephialtes pushed Otus aside. "But Otus thinks

the best way to capture a prisoner is to bind him with iron and tie him to a tree," he said.

"Well, that might work for a while. But what happens when the iron rusts and someone chops down the tree? Your prisoner will then be able to go free," Mars declared.

"Oh, great god of war! You are so much wiser than we. Show us—how would you capture a prisoner and keep him for all of eternity?" Otus and Ephialtes asked.

Mars showed them his special prison. It was a sealed room with no windows or doors. He showed them how to wrap a prisoner in chains of brass that would never unravel or rust.

Otus and Ephialtes watched, listened, and learned.

That night, when Mars was asleep, the twins secretly and silently wrapped him in his own brass chains. Then they dragged him across the room and threw him into his very own prison.

When Mars awoke, he realized that Otus and Ephialtes had tricked him. Mars was furious. He strained and struggled against his own chains with all his might. But even he did not have the strength to break the bonds of the gods.

Mars lay there in prison in despair. He was ashamed and surprised that mere mortals had gotten the best of him, a god. He did not know what to do.

Otus and Ephialtes laughed wildly the whole way home.

Jupiter learned what had happened to Mars. He became enraged. Jupiter wanted to declare war against the twins. But Mercury, his favorite son, convinced Jupiter that starting a war would be unwise.

"These giants are not mere mortals. Their strength is equal to ours. I will find a way to free Mars without them knowing. Then there will be no need for a war," Mercury told him.

Mercury rescued Mars in secret. Mars refused to speak of what happened.

Meanwhile, Otus and Ephialtes had come up with another trick to play on the gods.

They planned to stack the two highest mountains in the land on top of each other to reach the bottom of Mount Olympus. Then they would be able to climb Mount Olympus and take over the kingdom of the gods.

When Jupiter learned of this plan, he raged even more than before. He reached for his mighty thunderbolt. He readied himself to strike the twins where they stood. Just then, Neptune rose up from the sea.

"Brother, please, leave my sons be. They are young. They are foolish. I will teach them to behave," Neptune promised Jupiter.

For a moment, Jupiter did not want to consider the request. Then he saw how deeply Neptune loved his sons.

"I will not punish them . . . this time. But if anything else should happen, there will be nothing you can say or do to keep them alive," Jupiter warned.

Neptune scolded his twin giant sons.

"I've persuaded Jupiter not to harm you. You must behave from this day forward. If you play pranks, plot schemes, or embarrass the gods in any way, you will suffer."

Otus and Ephialtes promised Neptune that they would be good. But as soon as Neptune returned to the sea, the twins began plotting their next trick against the gods.

"I am in love with the goddess Juno," said Otus. "I would like her to be my queen bride."

"And I am in love with the huntress Diana," Ephialtes sighed.

"Let's steal them away and marry them," Otus declared.

"Who shall we take first?" Ephialtes asked.

"Let's draw straws," said Otus. "The short one wins," he announced.

The brothers drew straws to choose which goddess to steal first.

"I win!" exclaimed Ephialtes as he drew the shorter straw. "We will hunt for Diana first!"

The twin giant brothers did not know that Mercury had overheard them.

Mercury flew as fast as his winged sandals would take him. He went to warn Diana about the evil plan. She listened to Mercury's story of what he had overheard. Diana then came up with a plan of her own.

The twin giant brothers grabbed their hunting gear. They set out for the forest where Diana lived.

Diana waited till Otus and Ephialtes were in her sight. Then she jumped out in front of them and raced through the forest. The twins chased after her. Diana made them chase her all over.

But Diana was too quick for them. She led them between the trees. She steered them around giant boulders. She brought them all the way to the sea.

Diana knew that Neptune's sons could run on water as easily as they ran on land. She had them chase her across the ocean to the magical wooded island of Naxos. The island was not very big. Otus and Ephialtes were convinced they would catch her there.

"We are almost upon her. I have her in my sights!" Ephialtes called to Otus.

Just as the twin giant brothers closed in on Diana—she vanished!

But then the brothers saw a flash of white on the other side of the forest.

"Look—there!" Otus pointed to a beautiful milky-white deer springing through the trees. The deer turned and raced deeper into the woods.

Otus and Ephialtes were struck by the beauty of the creature. They forgot all about their chase after Diana.

The two giants crashed through the forests. They could think of nothing else but catching that beautiful white deer.

After a long time, the brothers were still not close to catching the deer.

"Let's separate and circle around the forest. We'll double our chances of catching the deer. I'll take the south path," Otus said.

"And I'll head north," Ephialtes said.

They each circled halfway around the woods. At the exact same moment, they saw it! The beautiful white deer stood still in the middle of an open glade. Otus stood on one side of the glade. Ephialtes stood on the other side. The deer was more radiant than either of them remembered. Its white fur seemed to glow. Neither brother saw that they stood opposite each other.

Their view across the glade was blocked by the magnificent deer.

Otus raised his spear. Ephialtes raised his at the same moment.

"One . . . two . . . three!" Each brother threw his spear at the deer with great force.

Suddenly the deer vanished from sight. The spears still traveled across the open glade. They found their marks.

Otus and Ephialtes crashed to the ground at the same time. Each brother was stabbed by the spear of the other.

The gods had finally had their revenge.

What Do *You* Think?
Questions for Discussion

♄

Have you ever been around a toddler who keeps asking the question "Why?" Does your teacher call on you in class with questions from your homework? Do your parents ask you about your day at the dinner table? We are always surrounded by questions that need a specific response. But is it possible to have a question with no right answer?

The following questions are about the book you just read. But this is not a quiz! They are designed to help you look at the people, places, and events from different angles. These questions do not have specific answers. Instead, they might make you think of these stories in a completely new way.

Think carefully about each question and enjoy discovering more about these classic myths.

1. In the story "The Oak and the Linden Tree," Baucis and Philemon are poor people with rich hearts. How does their behavior serve them when they encounter Jupiter and Mercury in disguise? Do you think the old man and woman would have behaved differently if they knew they were in the presence of two gods?

2. Both Prometheus and Io find themselves in terrible situations. How are their punishments similar? How are they different? Do you think either once deserves the torment?

3. Hercules thinks his eleventh labor—to steal the golden apples from the Garden of

the Hesperides—is absolutely impossible, even though he has already completed ten impossible tasks. How does Hercules complete his eleventh labor? Do you think he uses more of his strength or his brains to complete this task?

4. Romulus and Remus are twin brothers, but are they alike in any way besides looks? How are they different? Would Rome be different if it had been created and ruled by Remus?

5. Romulus and Remus are raised by a she-wolf who loves and protects them as if they were her own. Do you think this is strange? Have you ever heard of an animal coming to the aid of an animal of another species?

6. In Carthage, Aeneas and Dido fall in love through the power of Cupid's arrow. Do you think they would have fallen in love without the gods' magic? Would Aeneas have been able to sail to Italy without Dido's help? Do you think Aeneas wanted to leave Dido?

7. Aeneas finds out that his future descendants will create the city of Rome. Do you think this knowledge will affect his future actions? Do you think he now feels responsible for generations of men and women?

8. In the story "Cupid and Psyche," Psyche's curiosity overcomes her. What happens as a result? Would you be content to remain in the dark and be pampered? Or would you be curious enough to try and find out the truth?

9. In "Minerva and Arachne," the maiden Arachne angers the goddess Minerva and pays dearly for it. What exactly is her crime? Do you think her punishment fits her crime?

10. Otus and Ephialtes, the twin giants, also are punished for angering the gods. How exactly does their pride and mischief get them into trouble? In this story, Diana turns herself into a deer in order to trap the giants. What do you think the significance of this animal is?

A Note to Parents and Educators

By Arthur Pober, EdD

❧

First impressions are important.

Whether we are meeting new people, going to new places, or picking up a book unknown to us, first impressions can count for a lot. They can lead to warm, lasting memories or can make us shy away from future encounters.

Can you recall your own first impressions and earliest memories of reading the classics?

Do you remember wading through pages and pages of text to prepare for an exam? Or were you the child who hid under the blanket to read with a flashlight, joining forces with Robin Hood to save Maid Marian? Do you remember only how long it took you to read a lengthy novel such as *Little Women*? Or did you become best friends with the March sisters?

Even for a gifted young reader, getting through long chapters with dense language can easily become overwhelming and can obscure the richness of the story and its characters. Reading an abridged, newly crafted version of a classic novel can be the gentle introduction a child needs to explore the characters and story line without the frustrations of difficult vocabulary and complex themes.

Reading an abridged version of a classic novel gives the young reader a sense of independence and the satisfaction of finishing a "grown-up" book. And when a child is engaged with and inspired by a classic story, the tone is set for further exploration of the story's themes, characters, history, and details. As a child's reading skills advance, the desire to tackle the original, unabridged version of the story will naturally emerge.

If made accessible to young readers, these stories can become invaluable tools for understanding themselves in the context of their families and social environments. This is why the Classic Starts series includes questions that stimulate discussion regarding the impact and social relevance of the characters and stories today. These questions can foster lively conversations between children and their parents or teachers. When we look at the issues, values, and standards of past times in terms of how we live now, we can appreciate literature's classic tales in a very personal and engaging way.

Share your love of reading the classics with a young child, and introduce an imaginary world real enough to last a lifetime.

Dr. Arthur Pober, EdD

Dr. Arthur Pober has spent more than twenty years in the fields of early childhood and gifted education. He is the former principal of one of the world's oldest laboratory schools for gifted youngsters, Hunter College Elementary School, and former director of Magnet Schools for the Gifted and Talented for more than twenty-five thousand youngsters in New York City.

Dr. Pober is a recognized authority in the areas of media and child protection and is currently the US representative to the European Institute for the Media and European Advertising Standards Alliance.

Explore These Wonderful Stories in Our
Classic Starts™ Library.

20,000 Leagues Under the Sea

The Adventures of Huckleberry Finn

The Adventures of Robin Hood

The Adventures of Sherlock Holmes

The Adventures of Tom Sawyer

Alice in Wonderland & Through the Looking Glass

Animal Stories

Anne of Avonlea

Anne of Green Gables

Arabian Nights

Around the World in 80 Days

Ballet Stories

Black Beauty

The Call of the Wild

Dracula

The Five Little Peppers and How They Grew

Frankenstein

Great Expectations